W9-DES-085

To
Julia
Enjoy!
Jean E Navarra-Gibbons
1-25-01

WILLOWOOD

WILLOWOOD

Jean E. Navarra

VANTAGE PRESS
New York • Los Angeles

Illustrated by Sean Delonas

FIRST EDITION

All rights reserved, including the right of
reproduction in whole or in part in any form.

Copyright © 1990 by Jean E. Navarra

Published by Vantage Press, Inc.
516 West 34th Street, New York, New York 10001

Manufactured in the United States of America
ISBN: 0-533-08923-9

Library of Congress Catalog Card No.: 89-90574

1 2 3 4 5 6 7 8 9 0

To Paul and Janene

CONTENTS

WILLOWOOD

1.   *THE CITY*

There is a city in the world. It's a large, dark place with dirty streets and damp alleyways. The houses are small and old and strung together in long rows. Occasionally one can see a small clump of scraggly withered trees hovered above a cracked concrete bench. These little spots are called parks. Almost everyone who lives in the city works in a factory. There are many factories here. They are large and dingy-looking buildings with almost no windows. On top of the factories are smoke stacks. Black odorous smoke is continuously pouring out of them, making everything in the city dirty. Even on a bright sunny day, there is a gray haze in the air.

The main streets of the city are lined with shops of all kinds. They have large glass fronts that display their wares to those passing by. Ancient signs hang above each store in assorted sizes and colors, adding a bright spot to the city.

There are cars and buses and trains here. There are schools and movie theatres and a library. There are many people, places, and things. The city blends them all into its dark haze. Many small neighborhoods are pressed together like ragged pieces of an old puzzle.

In a tiny corner of the city, on the smallest of puzzle pieces, live two very special children.

2.   *JENNIFER AND DANIEL*

It was early November. The gray sky was streaked with the colors of the setting sun. Another chilly and damp day that made going out to play a definite "No!" with Mommy. That didn't stop Jennifer and Daniel from pressing their noses against the window that looked out onto their back yard. A small cracked patch of cement stared back at them. It was dotted with plastic flower pots and old toys.

"I want to go outside," said Daniel. He was six.

"Mommy won't let us, and besides, it's getting late," answered an older, wiser, almost-eight Jennifer. They were tired of watching TV. "Let's read some books," suggested Jennifer.

In one corner of the shabby living room, a pile of books was stacked. They were old and worn and had been read hundreds of times, but the two children loved them just the same. Danny loved to look at the pictures as Jennifer told a story to go with them. Their favorites were tales of faraway places, farm life, and outer space. They often wondered what it would be like to run in the grass and climb trees or just lie in a field and stare up at the sky.

Jennifer and Daniel lived in the city. The only trees they ever saw were in a tiny park a few blocks from their home. Everything else was a sidewalk or a street. Sometimes Mommy would take them shopping or for a walk. They often browsed in the old stores that lined the main street of their neighborhood. A favorite stop was Mr. Kletter's candy store.

"Just one piece each," said Mommy, smiling. Oh, how their faces lit up to be able to choose from all that candy behind the glass doors!

"Dinner's ready," called Mommy. The children sat down to a simple but delicious meal of homemade soup and peanut butter and jelly sandwiches.

"Where's Daddy?" asked Daniel.

"He'll be home late tonight," said Mommy. Daddy often worked late—something about making ends meet. The children weren't sure about what it meant. They only knew that Mommy and Daddy loved them and that they were all happy together.

After dinner was bath time. Danny splashed water everywhere as he played with his bath toys. Mommy scolded with a laugh, "Oh, Danny! What a mess." Mommy scrubbed him clean and toweled him dry. When she was finished, Danny felt warm and drowsy. Then it was Jennifer's turn.

Soon they were both tucked in bed. "Read us a story, Mommy," they both clamored.

"All right, but just one. You two look very tired to me." Mommy read one of their favorites. Before the story was finished, Danny was fast asleep.

Jennifer was in a thoughtful mood. "Mommy," she asked, "what would it be like to live somewhere else?" she asked. "Sometimes I wish we could. I want to see the country and the ocean and mountains and everything." Jennifer was getting very excited. "I

want to see every kind of animal there is and every kind of tree. Mommy, there are so many places I want to see. Do you think I'll ever be able to see them all?"

"If you really want to, you will," she answered. Jennifer could see her mother's face becoming very serious. "If you think about beautiful things, those things will become real. All the places you would like to see and the things you want to do are in your imagination. Do you know what that is, Jenny?" Jennifer shook her head silently, her blue eyes becoming wider. "It's the place in your thoughts where anything can happen. You can make your own world in your imagination. Whatever you want to be, wherever you want to be, you can make it happen in your thoughts."

Mommy took Jennifer's hands in hers and said, "Tonight, as you drift off to sleep, think about what you would like to see and do. Make it part of your dreams." Then Mommy gave them each a kiss and turned out the light. Before she left the room, she turned and gave them a long and loving look.

Jennifer thought about what her mother said. She had pictures in her mind. They were beautiful pictures filled with every color imaginable. Jennifer looked over at her little brother, smiled at him, and with these wonderful thoughts enveloping her, fell into a deep, deep sleep.

3.   *THE DREAM*

It was a cold night. But they were not cold. It was
dark. But they could see perfectly well. They were
alone. But they were not afraid. Jennifer and Daniel
found themselves in the middle of a large field. The
lights from faraway houses twinkled through the
trees at the edge of the field. The sky was filled with
millions of stars. They were like crystals reflecting
the light of each other. It almost seemed as if one
could reach up and touch them. The children were
bathed in the light from this crystal sky.

"Where are we?" asked Danny.

"I don't know," said Jenny, "but I have a feeling
that we are supposed to be here." As they continued
to gaze up at this special night sky, there appeared
a thin sliver of light. It seemed to be coming closer
to them.

"Jennifer, do you see that? What is it?" Daniel
was getting very curious and excited. He grabbed
Jennifer's hand.

"Yes, I see it too," she cried. It was getting much
closer now, the field was becoming brighter and
brighter. The two small upturned faces were growing
more amazed each minute. "Danny, it looks like a
rope of some kind." This is exactly what it was. A

rope twisting in such a way that would make it very easy to climb. It spiraled ever closer, finally coming to rest right in front of them. "I think we're supposed to climb up," said Jennifer.

"Maybe we'd better ask Mommy," said Daniel, a little bit concerned.

Jennifer smiled at him. "I think Mommy would tell us that we could. In fact, I'm sure she would."

And so they began to climb. Danny went first so that Jennifer could help him if he needed it. The rope itself seemed to help them. It twisted itself into little steps and handholds. It shimmered and felt so good to touch. The field was shrinking beneath them. The stars twinkled ever closer.

After climbing for what seemed a long time, they reached the end. All that could be seen was rope and sky. The air smelled so good and clean. The two children didn't even think of what might happen next. They felt so good and were enjoying this beautiful experience. Suddenly, the rope gave them a little push. It was quickly coiling itself up from the bottom. When it reached them, it became a large sphere, then a crystal. With a final push, it disappeared in a huge burst of light.

Jennifer and Daniel started to move—slowly at first, then faster and faster. Clutching one another's hands, they flew through the sky. Strangely enough, they were flying feet first, their hair streaming out behind them, their shining faces gazing at the sky. Stars were moving above them in a blaze of swirling light. The two children were so happy. They laughed and cried out in wonderment, "Look at us!" Of course, there was no one to see them. They were far above the Earth. When they turned their heads to look below, they could see fewer and fewer lights.

Finally, after what seemed a very long time, they could see no lights at all. Only the stars kept them company, winking at them in a brilliant array of patterns and sizes.

One of the stars seemed to be getting larger. As it came closer to them, Jennifer and Daniel could see that it was the same crystal that had earlier been a rope. Again it was turning into a sphere, and the sphere was beginning to uncoil. Here again was their beautiful stepladder back to the Earth.

"We're starting to slow down," cried Daniel. Jennifer held his little hand tightly.

No longer was the sky a crystal-lit blue. The stars were fading. A brilliant sun was pushing the night away. Silhouetted against the crimson and purple of this new sky were two small children descending a thin spiral to a waiting Earth.

4.   *PRYN*

Bump! Thump! Two small bottoms landed on soft earth and grass. Jennifer and Daniel were in the middle of a small clearing. Tall trees of every kind surrounded them. Birds chirped happy little tunes. But what amazed them more than anything were the beautiful colors. The morning sky seemed to glaze everything with a special glow. The trees had a purple tinge to them. The grass had a golden glimmer. A deep crimson mist swirled slowly through this unreal landscape.

"Jennifer!" called Daniel.

"I'm right here," said a bewildered Jennifer. They were both still sitting on the soft tall grass.

"Where is this place?" asked Daniel. He wasn't afraid, but he knew he had never seen anything like this before.

"I don't know where we are," said Jennifer. "Maybe if we walk around a bit we'll see a sign or something." The two travelers got up and stretched. There was a clean scent in the misty air. They wandered slowly around the clearing. Their eyes were trying to see everything at once.

"This is really a nice place," said Daniel.

Jennifer laughed at him. "Oh Daniel, it's much

more than nice, it's the most wonderful place I've ever seen."

All at once they began to hear a faint sound. "Can you hear that?" said Jennifer.

"Yes," said Daniel, "I think it's music." A haunting little melody was drifting in on the mist. A high and reedy sound—not too different from the song of the birds.

"I wonder where it's coming from," they said in unison.

The forest itself must have heard their question. A path that led through the trees appeared right in front of them. "Look!" cried Jennifer. "Let's see where it takes us."

"Are you sure about this?" asked Daniel, his brown eyes getting larger.

"Just hold my hand," said Jennifer.

So off they went along the path. It unraveled as they went along much as the star-rope did. They could hear and sometimes see small furry woodland creatures scurrying about their business. The sound of the music grew stronger and prettier.

After a short while, the path ended. It led into another clearing. This spot was larger than the first one. In the middle of it was a large pond surrounded by rocks of all sizes and shapes. Jennifer and Daniel were gazing in awe at this beautiful scene when they were startled by a soft little voice behind them.

"So they found us at last," it said. The children spun around to see who might be speaking to them. On a large moss-covered rock to the right of the path

sat a tiny little man. They had never seen anyone like him before. He was much smaller than Daniel and the strangest sight they had ever seen. He was dressed in green from head to toe, including little green slippers and a tiny green cap. His eyes were a bright gold color. His ears were long and pointed. On his chin was a small beard. In his hands, the little creature held what looked like some kind of instrument. He had obviously been playing the music that they heard.

Daniel folded his arms across his chest and narrowed his eyes. "Are you a Martian?" he demanded.

"No! No! No!" the tiny man said softly, shaking his head with every repetition of the word.

"Daniel likes stories about outer space," apologized Jennifer. "But please tell us who you are—and," she added thoughtfully, "what you are."

The little man stood up gracefully, took off his cap revealing the brown curly hair under it, and bowed to them. "My name is Pryn," he said, looking at Jennifer, "and I am an elf," he informed Daniel.

5.   *WOODLAND JOURNEY*

Daniel was still very cautious about Pryn. He circled the elf a few times to make sure that he was real. Pryn smiled at Daniel, sat down on his rock, and played a little more of his melody. After staring in bewilderment for a few minutes, it occurred to Jennifer that the little being might be able to answer some questions for them.

"Could you please tell us where we are?" she asked as politely as possible.

"Of course," said Pryn in his soft small voice. "You have come to the world of Willowood. And you are quite near the Village," he added. This answer certainly didn't make matters any clearer to Jennifer.

"What is Willowood?" she asked.

Pryn looked very puzzled at this. "Oh, my goodness, they asked to come here but don't know where they are," Pryn mused to himself.

"I suppose you are both hungry and thirsty after your journey," he said at last. The children hadn't thought about food for a while, but now that they were reminded about it, yes, they were very hungry. "I can tell by your faces that I've hit upon just the thing you need—a good meal. Please follow me." As he said this, Pryn jumped down from his perch on the large rock. It looked to the two travelers like he floated down. He stood in front of them now, a strange but wonderful sight.

Pryn bowed again, put his instrument to his lips, and started to walk out of the clearing. They passed the glassy pond and approached the deep woods once more. Again a path cleared before them. Down this path the three traveled. Pryn, in front, sometimes did a funny little hop as he walked. Jennifer and Daniel were too busy looking around to notice Pryn's little dance. This was the most unusual place they had ever seen. The trees were tall and straight. The forest floor was carpeted with leaves of every color, which sparkled when patches of golden sunlight warmed them. Although it was a sunny day, a silvery mist drifted through the trees. Everything around them glittered with soft color.

There were small (and not so small) woodland creatures in this forest of Willowood. Jennifer and Daniel hadn't seen too many animals in the City. Even the pictures of animals in their many books could not compare with these strange animals. Birds of the most beautiful colors flew through the trees. Some even perched on nearby branches to watch them.

Finally, Jennifer's curiosity got the better of her. "Mr. Pryn," she called. The soft melody stopped as Pryn turned and smiled at her. "What kind of animals live here? They don't look like any animals I've ever seen."

Daniel piped in, "Do they bite?"

14

Pryn's response made them feel much safer. "There are no dangerous animals in Willowood these days." As he spoke, his golden eyes grew larger. "You have come to a place where animals live in peace with all who dwell here. Because of this, many different kinds of animals have remained and new kinds have come into being."

Jennifer wasn't too sure that she understood all of this. Pryn noticed her puzzled look and said, "I'll explain more as we continue our journey." Now that he knew the animals were tame, Daniel immediately tried to catch one. "All that you have to do is call him," said Pryn softly.

Daniel stood in disbelief for a moment. Then, with a shrug, he called out to a small furry animal peeking around a tree, "Please come here." A black furry creature no bigger than a cat came scurrying up to him. Daniel picked it up and hugged it. Two big purple eyes looked up at him. "He's so cute." Daniel was delighted. After a minute of cuddling in Daniel's arms, the little animal jumped down and scampered away. "Where is he going?" Daniel was disappointed.

"Even animals have places to go and things to do," explained Pryn. "He will come to you again, I'm sure."

The trio again turned their attention to the path unfolding before them. It seemed that they had walked for quite a while when Pryn stopped and said, "We have come to the Village—my village. I welcome you!"

6.   *THE VILLAGE*

Without warning, the forest ended. Beyond the trees was a large, grass-covered valley. Small shrubs and flowers grew in spots here and there. The vegetation was unfamiliar to the children, especially the flowers. They were large and glittered like jewels. Even the grass was different from what little grass they had ever seen. It was like a thick springy carpet, soft to their feet but never getting trampled.

Daniel started to run and jump with excitement. He did cartwheels and tumbles and simply rolled everywhere. Jennifer ran to the nearest clump of flowers to admire them. "Do you pick these flowers?" she asked breathlessly.

"Oh, no!" answered Pryn, his golden eyes growing larger. "We let them live in the ground where we can enjoy their beauty for a long time."

Now Daniel came running back to them. "Jennifer, look at the little houses." At the bottom of the valley, they could see a large number of tiny huts. They were all made of rough hewn stone, but no two were alike. Some were longer than others, with more windows. Others had small signs hung over their round oaken doors. The windows of these elfin cottages were made of a curious kind of glass that sparkled like jewels in the deep orange sunlight. There were narrow pathways paved with stone throughout the village.

They had just come to one of these pathways when Jennifer said, "It looks like a beautiful fairyland."

Pryn laughed and replied, "It's a beautiful elfin village. The fairies have their own place." The children could see other elves in the Village. They were walking up and down the pathways or sitting in front of their cottages playing instruments much like Pryn's.

They waved and greeted Jennifer and Daniel as they passed saying, "Welcome to the Village!"

"Do they know who we are?" asked Daniel.

"Oh, yes," said Pryn, "I told them you were coming."

Daniel was very puzzled by this answer. "How did you know we were coming? We didn't even know it."

Pryn winked at Daniel. "I always know when children need me," he said softly and seriously. Pryn now stopped in front of a small hut at the end of one of the pathways. Again he bowed to them. "This is my home. Please come in and refresh yourselves."

7.   *PRYN'S HUT*

It wasn't a very large home, but the children were very comfortable. Because they were children, they were small enough to fit nicely on Pryn's furniture. All of the elf's furniture was made of hand-carved wood sanded to a silky, smooth finish. The cushions were made of a hand-woven material, stuffed with what felt like straw. Along one of the walls was a large fireplace with chunky logs in it crackling quietly and giving a warm soft glow to the room.

A small stairway led to a loft. This was Pryn's bedroom. Daniel was a curious little boy. He explored the hut from top to bottom, examining every detail and utensil. "I like this place," he declared with a big smile.

"I am happy that my home pleases you," said Pryn. Jennifer was more interested in the view from the back windows of Pryn's hut. A large stream sparkled not far away. It wound its way through the village in both directions as far as Jennifer could see. "I see that you have noticed our stream," said Pryn.

Jennifer turned around and smiled. "It's beautiful and so long. I can't see where it goes."

"Oh, but you will," he said with a twinkle in his

golden eyes. Jennifer was puzzled, but at that moment she caught sight of the meal laid out on the elf's table.

While the children were exploring their surroundings, Pryn was busy preparing a meal. Fresh fruit, cheeses, hot biscuits, and milk were waiting for them. Everything was arranged in hand-carved wooden bowls and cups.

Neither Jennifer nor Daniel realized just how hungry they were until they sat down at Pryn's table to eat. "Boy, this is good stuff," said Daniel as he munched a large piece of cheese.

"This is the best milk I've ever had," said Jennifer with a sigh.

When they were finished, they helped Pryn clear the table and put away the remaining food. Pryn then invited them to sit close to the fireplace. There were large cushions for them and a small stool for Pryn. The children listened quietly while Pryn played his instrument. His music wasn't like anything they had ever heard.

After a while, Pryn put his instrument away and said, "Would you like to know why you are here?"

"Yes," they answered in unison.

"Well, I'll tell you," Pryn stated softly. "I can hear the unspoken wishes of all children. It is my special gift to know when children are not entirely happy with a situation. Then I call them to me and give them the tools to change their lives."

With a thoughtful look on his face, Daniel said, "I don't remember anybody calling me."

"Neither do I," chimed in Jennifer, "but Mommy said I could dream of what I wanted, and it would happen. Are we dreaming?" she asked, her eyes wide with this possibility.

"Yes, you are dreaming," said Pryn. He went on to explain. "Dreams are a very special part of you. Sometimes you can find the answer to a problem in a dream. In dreams you enter into a world where all things are possible. And if the dream is strong enough, it will become part of your waking life."

"Is that what Mommy meant?" asked Jennifer.

"Yes," said Pryn, smiling. "Your mother is a wise woman."

"But we're not unhappy really," said Daniel, his long dark hair almost in his large brown eyes.

"You have parents who love you and take care of you as best they can," said Pryn. "In this respect you are the luckiest children in the world. However, wishes and yearnings come in many forms. I help children with all their problems and desires. All children have different lives and different dreams. Their dreams are the future of your world. All these lives and dreams will intertwine to create a future of some kind. It is my wish that this future will be a good one. I can help you to create your own happiness and destiny. For each child that I help, the possibilities become better for your world."

Daniel looked a little sad after hearing this. "I'm just a little boy. How can I help the great big world?"

Pryn was very serious now. "Everyone is equally important in helping their world. You are just as necessary to the future as the most important adult."

Jennifer took his hand in hers. She realized just how much she loved her little brother. "We'll learn together, Daniel, and I'll help you to understand"— Jennifer paused for a moment—"after Pryn helps me to understand."

Pryn laughed softly. "I'll help you both to learn. You are both special with strong minds and vivid imaginations. It will be a pleasure to accompany you on your journey."

"Where are we going?" asked Daniel, becoming excited again.

"Many places," answered Pryn quietly, "many places."

8. *THE PLAN*

It was twilight in Willowood. If you walked along the pathways of the Village, you would see firelight coming through the windows of each hut. You would hear soft music as the elves played their handmade instruments. Small lights began to twinkle in the trees. The last of the sunset remained in the sky as crimson and purple streaks. A deep and beautiful calm could be felt in this magic and mysterious land.

Just beyond the last row of huts in the village, a clear stream wound its way through the forest. Small boats were secured here and there along part of this stream. One of these boats belonged to an elf named Pryn.

"I will tell you my plan," said Pryn. "We will make a journey down the stream. There are many thousands of streams in Willowood. They all lead to the River. Many kinds of creatures live in my world. They all have a job to do—a part to play in helping your world and other worlds to become all that they can be. Each has their own stream that leads to the River. The streams of Willowood are its life blood. The River is the major artery that leads to the heart of Willowood—The Great Castle. That is where we will go. The many lessons you will learn along the way will prepare you for the greatest lesson of all. Then you will return to your own world, your own reality, and make it a better place because of what you have learned."

Jennifer and Daniel were quite bewildered by what they were hearing. They were also very excited about what was happening to them. Pryn disappeared for a few minutes. When he returned, he was carrying two small bundles. "You can't make the journey comfortably in your bedroom clothes," he said with a grin. The two children had never even thought about it, but yes, they were still in their pajamas. Pryn handed a bundle to each of them. Daniel opened his immediately. His bundle contained a long shirt and a pair of pants. Also, there were sturdy shoes and thick socks to go with them. Jennifer's parcel contained a blouse, skirt, shoes, and long stockings. All these things were made of the same material as Pryn's and were, of course, green.

The clothing was a perfect fit for both of them. "This stuff is really neat," said Daniel as he marched around the room.

Jennifer was equally delighted with her outfit. "It feels like very strong material," she said, smoothing out the pretty skirt.

"Yes," answered Pryn, "it is designed for all kinds of travel and any kind of weather."

Pryn said, "I will pack something for us to eat for the first part of our journey, and then we can begin. Our first stop will be made in about two days' time—two Willowood days, that is."

"How long is a Willowood day?" asked Jennifer.

"As long as we want it to be or as short. Time is different here," he explained. "It will be your minds and imaginations that determine your stay at each point in this experience."

Two sets of large, bright eyes stared into Pryn's golden ones. They were starting to get an idea of what a special place this was.

Daniel was curious about something. "Don't we have to get some sleep now?"

"No," said Pryn matter-of-factly.

"Why not?" asked Jennifer.

"You are asleep." Pryn was smiling his funny little smile. Jennifer and Daniel looked at each other. What an amazing place to be. And what a wonderful dream to be dreaming.

9. *THE MEDALLION*

Three small figures carrying three small knapsacks emerged from the back of Pryn's hut. They walked down a short path. At the end of the path was Pryn's boat. It wasn't a very large one, but they fit in it quite comfortably. Pryn untied the sturdy rope from the post and pushed them gently away from the shore.

"Before we start," said Pryn, "I have something to give you." In the night Pryn's eyes glowed with a special light. The children watched him now as he reached into one of his pockets. He pulled out two round objects, each of them attached to a chain. "These medallions are worn by all who visit Willowood. Anyone who sees them will know that you have been invited here." Pryn handed each of them a medallion. They were round and had something engraved on the front of them. Pryn explained what these engravings were.

"In the middle of the medallion, you will see the Great Castle. The W's on each side stand for Willowood. There is also a moon, a star, and a sun." Pryn's voice was so gentle that it almost blended in with the murmuring stream. But because of its gentleness, the two children listened very attentively.

They were coming to love this little creature in a very special way.

Pryn continued, "The Great Castle is the heart of all wisdom in Willowood. The moon, stars, and sun symbolize the timelessness of true wisdom."

"I don't think I understand this at all," said Daniel with a sigh. The little boat was rocking gently. The sun had set long ago, but the scene was softly lit by a large full moon. The trees that lined the stream sparkled with small lights of their own.

In this calm and unique light, a part of Jennifer was becoming aware of the meaning of this rare dream. "Everyone has a heart," she said quietly, more to herself than to Pryn and Daniel. "If we can discover the meaning of the Great Castle, or heart of Willowood, then maybe we will understand what is in our own hearts." Now she looked up at Pryn. "And if we understand our own hearts, that understanding will help us at any time in our lives."

"Yes! Yes! Yes!" said Pryn. He was smiling at them but serious at the same time.

Daniel looked at his big sister. "How do we know what's in our hearts?"

"I think we're going to learn that in Willowood," she answered.

Pryn now asked them to put the medallions around their necks. Even though they were made of stone, they were not heavy. The Castle glittered and so did the other symbols. They sparkled with every color at once. The children now felt that they were ready for anything they might encounter on their journey.

"I see that you are ready," said Pryn softly. As he said this, he bent over and knocked three times on the bottom of the boat. Daniel and Jennifer looked at each other, then at Pryn.

"Why did you do that?" asked Daniel.

"You'll see," said Pryn, winking at him. They were moving! Slowly at first, then a little faster.

"What's moving us?" asked Jennifer. "We're not rowing and we don't have a motor."

Pryn just sat there, his small arms folded. He was amused at their bewilderment. Finally he said, "Look over the side. What do you see?" Daniel looked over one side and Jennifer the other.

There were lights everywhere. Small, flickering lights darting this way and that under the dark water. "What are they?" Daniel cried.

"They're so beautiful," said Jennifer with awe.

"They are very special fish," answered Pryn proudly. "They are creating a current that carries us along. They also light our way at night. All the creatures of Willowood are quite special. We all help each other out in many ways."

After their initial excitement gave way to a more calm feeling, the two travelers talked together and with Pryn about the unusual things that they were seeing. Pryn would pick up his little instrument now and then and play a tune. Eventually the sky began to lighten. Again the surrounding countryside took on the morning colors that were unique to Willowood. The boat continued to move, but the fish could no longer be seen.

10. LANDSCAPE

The new morning light sparkled on a very different scene for the journeyers. During the night the landscape slowly changed from a forest to large fields.

"Everything looks so different today," exclaimed Jennifer.

"Where are all the trees and stuff?" asked Daniel, looking all around.

Pryn smiled a little smile and said, "Every day brings something new to those who travel in this land. Just as every day in your lives you learn something new or understand something old in a new way. Your minds create a fresh canvas to be painted every day."

They listened very attentively to Pryn. The children were really beginning to understand the elf's way of explaining ideas. Again they turned their attention to the scenes around them. The fields were yellow. The grass was very long. Here and there they could see the grass part.

"What's happening over there?" asked Daniel as he stood up and slightly rocked the little boat. "I wish we could get out and walk around," he added. Immediately the small craft slowed down and drifted to a low slope on the shore. "Did the fish hear me?" asked Daniel in amazement.

"All of Willowood heard you," answered Pryn. His soft voice was like the whisper of the grass as it rustled in a gentle breeze. "Something I think you should remember," Pryn said as they pulled the boat up on shore, "you may need it sometime soon. In the dream world of Willowood, I am your guide, but it is your wishes and your desires that will be fulfilled. You may change the dream."

"Why would we want to change something so beautiful?" asked Jennifer.

"Your heart will tell you why as we continue our journey," Pryn answered mysteriously. Jennifer and Daniel looked at each other. They knew Pryn well enough to know that what he said was always important, and they remembered his words.

The small travelers and their guide climbed the low slope and stood at the edge of the field. It seemed to be endless, broken only by a few large rock formations. Daniel now pointed to one of these formations. "Let's see what's over there."

Just as it had in the forest, the grass parted to make a path for them. The sun cast an orange glow to everything. The air had an autumnlike quality about it. As they approached the rock, the grass got shorter until it was like a deep yellow carpet.

"It's so soft here," said a delighted Jennifer. Beside the rock was a small but deep pond of the freshest water.

"You have made a wise choice, my boy," said Pryn. "Here we can have a small meal and rest a bit." As he said this, he sat down, opened his knapsack and began to unwrap something. He looked up at the children. "Would you like to join me?" he asked softly. Jennifer and Daniel were quite ready for something to eat.

"Tell me something, Pryn," said Jennifer. "If we don't need to sleep, why do we need to eat anything?"

"That is a very good question," said Pryn in his quiet little voice. "This food is for the soul, or spirit, or imagination. It's for the part of you that's not material."

"What does that mean?" asked a very curious Daniel.

Pryn went on, "The material part of you is what you can see—arms, legs, feet, hands, head—do you see what I mean?"

"Yes," said Daniel. He was looking at himself, straining his neck to see his chest.

Jennifer began to laugh at him. "Sometimes you're such a funny little brother."

And so they ate a meal of fruit and bread and cheese, and drank some of the fresh water. Pryn played a pretty little song for them. The children felt deeply rested and very happy.

After a while, Daniel spotted the grass parting a short distance from where they sat. It was coming towards them. "I think we're going to have a visitor," said Pryn smiling.

Daniel stood up to see better. "It's almost here, it's almost here." He was very excited. Finally, emerging from the tall grass was the strangest animal they had ever seen.

It stood in front of them now and made a small

sound as if to say hello. Jennifer just stared at the animal in disbelief. She wasn't sure if it was dangerous or not, but Daniel remembered what Pryn had said about all animals living in peace in Willowood. He walked closer to the strange beast. "What is it?" he asked quite simply and with no fear.

Pryn smiled at both of them and exclaimed proudly, "That is a Willopede!" When the Willopede heard Pryn's voice, it came to him and gave him a playful little nudge. "These fields are the home of the Willopede. Other animals also dwell in this part of Willowood, but you will find this particular animal in great numbers. The yellow grass is what they like to eat."

The Willopede was mostly yellow because of its diet. It had six sturdy legs, a long tail, and large orange eyes. Its face was a bit like a cat and a monkey mixed together. A small whirring noise came from it every once in a while.

"What's he saying?" asked Daniel.

"He wants to know if he can say hello to you," answered Pryn.

"How does a Willopede say hello?" asked Daniel a bit cautiously.

"You'll see," said Pryn, laughing softly. "He won't hurt you." The animal trotted over to Daniel, gave him a gentle nudge, and made his little "whirr."

Daniel smiled. "He's kind of cute in a weird sort of way."

"Very weird," Jennifer agreed. She was beginning to warm up to the Willopede.

After it made its hellos to everyone, the Willopede went to get a drink from the pond. It then went back to the path it had made, nudging everyone on the way, made a louder whirr, and disappeared in the field once more. "What a neat animal," said Daniel, jumping up and down.

Jennifer sat down and said more to herself than anyone, "This is a very unusual place." Pryn just laughed and did his little dance.

Once more, night was coming to Willowood. In the last light of a purple twilight, Pryn made a small fire. It wasn't cold, but the fire gave a warm glow to the little clearing and the shadow of the flames danced beautifully on the rock formation. The two children sat and reflected on the day's happenings.

"I'm very happy that we stopped off here," said Jennifer.

"Me too!" said a very happy Daniel.

Pryn stopped playing his instrument (which, by the way, is called a moonflute because it is shaped like a ball and has holes in many places) and said quietly, "Now it is time to move on." Jennifer and Daniel felt the same way. They didn't know why, but they knew Pryn was right.

From the shore and hidden out of sight, the Willopede watched two small children and an even smaller elf climb into a tiny boat. It made a quiet little whirr as the flickering lights of the fish moved the boat down the stream.

Overlooking all of them was a blanket of crystal stars, sparkling in the deep purple sky.

11.   *THE ROCK*

A large bright moon and millions of stars now lit the
scene of the journey. The landscape was beginning
to change again. What had been a few large rock
formations in the fields were becoming more numer-
ous. Gradually, the banks of the stream became solid
rock. Not a sheer wall of rock, but many different
kinds and colors. Some rocks were so large that it
was impossible to see the end of them. Others fit
together to form fantastic arrangements. There were
crystal rocks that sparkled and glittered in the moon-
light, and huge gemstones with their own deep, rich
colors. It was a sight that could only exist in Willowood.

For the most part, Jennifer and Daniel sat in
silence. They were in awe of their new surroundings.
Occasionally one of them would exclaim, "Look at
that one!" or "Look at the color of this. Pryn, what
is it?"

Pryn would put his moonflute down for a minute
and answer, "That is an emerald," or, "That is a rose
quartz stone." Pryn, as usual, was enjoying their
amazement at the unique variety that was Willowood.

Eventually, they came to a bend in the stream.

As they rounded the bend, they could see something glowing in the distance. It was a large rock—a blue one that looked like a neon sign pulsing in the night.

Daniel was quick to ask, "Are we going to stop there?"

"Yes," said Pryn softly, "we are going to see Cyrus."

"Who is Cyrus?" asked Jennifer.

Pryn answered matter-of-factly, "He is the Spacer-Time explorer of Willowood. I will let him explain what he does." This was an unusual answer for Pryn, and it made the children very curious indeed.

As they came closer to this special rock, the flicker-fish came to a slow stop. "Why are we stopping? We're not there yet." Daniel was excited again. Pryn's answer was a silent smile and eyes that sparkled in the blue glow.

"How are we going to get in there?" asked Jennifer. The question was a good one because the rock looked solid from top to bottom. Her question was answered in a very unusual way. But, after all, the unusual was always happening in Willowood.

A large flickering light was moving in their direction under the water. It looked like it came from under the blue rock. It was a much larger light than the light of their tiny navigator fish, and it stopped right in front of the boat. A tiny head popped out of the water. A small high-pitched voice said, "Welcome to the home of Cyrus. I will lead you in from here."

"Who are you?" said Jennifer. Needless to say,

the children were amazed at this new wonder.

"I am Nami. I am a river sprite." Nami had very short curly hair that glittered with tiny gems. This is what made her glow under the water. She disappeared quickly. The navigator fish began to move again, following Nami to the blue rock. As they came up to the rock, a part of it swung open. The boat was being guided into a large dark tunnel.

"I don't know if I like this," said Jennifer. "I can't see anything."

"Would you like to see where you are?" asked Pryn.

"Yes, I would," she answered. Then she remembered what to do. "I would like to see where we are." Jennifer spoke in a firm, clear voice. At once the walls of the tunnel began to glow with the same blue light as the outside of it. They could see Nami and the fish under the dark water.

Soon they rounded a bend. Up ahead was an enormous bridge. There were steps leading from the water to this structure on either side. Leaning over a stone railing, watching their approach, was Cyrus. "Hello! Hello!" he cried out. "Come up to my home, please. There is much here to see and learn." He had a quick and kindly voice.

They had now come to the bottom of one set of steps. The boat stopped, and Pryn secured it to a post with a sturdy rope. Little Nami jumped out and scampered up the steps, her hair sparkling. Now they could see the rest of her. She was pale blue and wore a shiny blue bathing suit. Her little feet were webbed

and looked like tiny flippers. She looked behind her and said, "Come up! Come up!" She then jumped onto a small outcropping of rock that looked like a seat made just for her.

Up the stairs they went. First Daniel, then Jennifer, and then Pryn. "Well, well, you must be Daniel, and you must be Jennifer," said Cyrus. He shook hands with each of them.

Pryn bowed to him and said to the children, "This is Cyrus." Cyrus was a tall, thin man with pale skin, blue hair and eyes that glowed like small blue light bulbs . . . in fact, all of him seemed to glow faintly.

With a large, sweeping gesture, Cyrus asked, "What do you think of my home?"

Jennifer and Daniel looked around. The bridge was large and made entirely of stone. One side looked over the water in the tunnel. The other side looked like it was built into the rock. The river flowed under them and out of sight. "There isn't anything here," said Jennifer in a doubtful voice.

"Where do you keep all your stuff?" asked Daniel.

"Ah, ha! You are very bright children," said Cyrus. "This is my front porch. My home is in here." As he spoke, Cyrus turned to the wall of rock behind them and placed the palm of his hand on it. A large part of the rock began to slide upward, revealing a brilliantly glowing interior of white and pale blue crystal. Cyrus turned proudly and said, "Welcome to my home and laboratory."

The children were blinking in the brightness of

the entranceway. "This is just like an ice palace I saw in a book once," said Jennifer. She was delighted, and so was Daniel who was running ahead of everyone. When they were all inside, the door slid shut.

"Wow! Look at this place," said Daniel. It was certainly something to see. There were many alcoves in this gigantic space. Each one had sets of control panels built right into the crystal rock. They blinked with many colors and were dotted with knobs and dials of all kinds. One of the rooms also contained plants in clear crystal vases from floor to ceiling. These plants were very strange in color and in shape.

Jennifer and Daniel wandered around, amazed and delighted in this fantastic place. Nami darted about laughing and chattering to herself.

Pryn stood beside Cyrus and said softly, "I have visited here many times, Cyrus, but your home becomes more beautiful with each visit."

"Thank you," said Cyrus with a short, quick bow. Cyrus was smiling at his visitors and anxious to explain his surroundings.

12. *THE SCREEN*

"Jennifer, come and look at this room," called Daniel. "It looks like a giant movie screen."

Jennifer joined him quickly. Cyrus and Pryn were right behind her.

"And so it is, my boy," said Cyrus. There was a large chair in front of a flat, square crystal that covered one wall of the room. A long control panel was twinkling in front of the chair. "This is a Time-Space viewer." Cyrus looked into two sets of puzzled eyes.

Sitting in the chair, he said, "I'll explain." He turned one of the dials on the control panel, and the room became very dark. Only the screen was lit. "With this device, I can see any place in the universe at any time in its history." Cyrus turned another dial. What appeared on the screen was so large and realistic that the children thought they were actually in it. "Don't be afraid," said Cyrus, "what you see on the screen has not been real on your planet for millions of years."

"Dinosaurs!" said Daniel. "I have books about them. Look how big they are," he said, reaching out his hand as if to touch an enormous toe.

"What happened to them?" asked Jennifer as she watched them move on the screen.

"No one really knows except me," said Cyrus

mysteriously. The children looked at him now. His hair and eyes were glowing in the dark room. "I have scanned the earth of this period, and I have seen what made them extinct."

"Oh, show us!" they both clamored.

Cyrus adjusted a dial. Immediately the scene changed. A large fiery object appeared in a dark sky. It hit the earth with such a force that it caused much destruction on the planet. They could see earthquakes and fires and climate changes taking place. "After the meteor struck, the dinosaurs could no longer survive," said Cyrus, turning another dial.

"The poor dinosaurs," said Jennifer sadly.

"Could it happen again?" asked Daniel. He was a little worried.

"Oh, it's possible," said Cyrus, "but very unlikely. The future holds an infinite variety of possibilities. I'm going to show you one of these possible futures." On the screen was a totally different scene. "This is the planet Altron III. It is a dying planet in a remote corner of the universe."

What the children saw on the screen was a sad and desolate sight. They could see dried-up ocean beds and deserts. There were no trees or other plants or animals. As the planet came closer on the screen, they could see what was left of the inhabitants of Altron III. It looked like they were all at a meeting. Food and water were being rationed to them in very small amounts. Most of them were carrying large knapsacks.

"It looks like they're all going on a trip," said Jennifer in a curious tone.

"Maybe they are," said Cyrus. "Let's scan the area and see if we can find out."

After a few seconds, Daniel cried out and pointed, "Look at that huge spaceship! I'll bet they're all going to leave the planet."

"Yes," said Cyrus, "I'm afraid that they have no choice."

The viewers watched as the people of Altron III boarded their ship. "They all look so sad," said Jennifer.

"You would be sad, too, if you had to leave earth to look for another home," said Cyrus.

"They're really neat looking," said Daniel. He was always interested in "outer space" and beings that might be out there. The Altronians were indeed a beautiful race of people. They were tall and slender with white hair and purple, almond-shaped eyes.

"I wonder how they made out," said Cyrus.

"What do you mean?" asked Jennifer.

"The scene you are watching took place about one thousand years ago," answered Cyrus. "Remember, we can view anywhere at anytime on this screen."

"Wow!" said Daniel to himself.

"I hope they found another home," said Jennifer. "And I sure hope it never happens to our earth," she added.

"That will be up to you," said Cyrus with a small smile.

"What can we do?" asked Daniel.

"Oh, there is much that you can do," said Cyrus. He got up from his chair and pushed a button. The room was bright again, and the scene disappeared from the crystal screen. "You can help to take care of your world," he continued. "You can conserve water, recycle certain materials, and respect all plant and animal life on earth. As you become adults, you will be part of the process that makes laws to protect your world."

"I guess the Altronians didn't do any of that stuff," said Daniel thoughtfully.

Cyrus became very serious. "It was too late to do anything once they realized their planet was in trouble. Only then did they come to know what they had lost."

As Cyrus and the children exchanged ideas about the fate of the Altronians, they moved into the plant room. Here they were surrounded by the most unusual variety of plant life that could be imagined. Jennifer and Daniel had come to believe that most plants were green. But in this room, that belief came to an end. There were plants, flowers, and shrubs of every color and shape. Some of them looked impossible—a bush made entirely of cube-shaped leaves, flowers with small, handlike roots that seemed to search and grab for food. They encountered many strange sights in this room.

"Cyrus, where do all of these things come from?" asked Jennifer in a voice filled with awe. Cyrus was leaning against a counter with his arms folded and a large grin on his glowing face.

"I've collected them from all parts of the Universe," he answered proudly.

"How did you do that?" asked Daniel doubtfully.

"Oh, that's easy," said Cyrus with a wave of his hands. "I simply make an adjustment to my crystal screen, press a button, and—aha!—there it is." As he explained this, Cyrus picked up a small clear vase with a beautiful blue tree so tiny that it could fit in Daniel's hand. "This is my favorite," he said in a sad voice. "Do you have any idea why?" His blue eyes began to fill with tears. Jennifer and Daniel looked at each other and then at Cyrus.

"Why is that one so special?" asked Jennifer.

"Because it came from my home planet a long time ago." Cyrus replaced the tree lovingly.

"Where do you come from?" asked Daniel with great interest.

"Oh, my planet isn't around anymore," said Cyrus, cheering up a bit. "The sun in my solar system began to die, so we had to leave, even though our planet was thriving. I came to Willowood in a small spacecraft made of crystal and made it my home."

"Wow!" said Daniel, looking all around, "is this a real spaceship?"

"Yes indeed, my boy. I suppose you could call it a mobile home." Cyrus laughed wildly, his eyes and hair glowing like blue fire.

Cyrus took the children on a tour of his fantastic home. They spent a great deal of time with this wise and kindly creature. They learned many things about the universe and gained a new respect for the Earth and all life on it.

13.   *BACK PORCH*

All at once it occurred to Daniel that he hadn't seen Pryn for quite some time. He looked around quickly, just to make sure, but no, Pryn was nowhere to be seen.

"What's the matter?" asked Jennifer.

"Where did Pryn go?" Daniel looked up at her.

Cyrus answered his question. "He and Nami are playing their insruments together on my back porch. Shall we say hello?"

With a touch of a button, one wall of the room slid up. Instead of a tunnel, they were greeted with daylight.

"Oh, how beautiful!" sighed Jennifer. Cyrus's "back porch," as he called it, was an outcropping of rose-colored crystal. It was enormous. Here and there were chairlike formations. Pryn and Nami were facing each other in two of these formations while they played their special music. Nami had a small crystal wind instrument, and of course, Pryn had his moonflute. The most wonderful sounds filled the air. Beyond the balcony they could see the stream rippling like a long blue ribbon. A bright sun added to the brilliance of the crystal and water. Traces of green were beginning to crop up between the crystals on the banks of the stream.

Pryn and Nami were so absorbed in their duet that they didn't notice the approach of their friends. Finally, it was Nami's little sparkling head that looked up. "Hello, hello!" she cried, running up to them, "We're going to have a picnic."

"We are?" said Jennifer, looking around doubtfully.

"Of course we are,"said Cyrus, and he produced a large basket from behind a chair formation. "Let's all sit at my large table." They followed Cyrus to a large round crystal surrounded by many smaller ones. Here they sat down to a meal of the most unusual foods imaginable. Most of it was from Cyrus's home planet, including a clear blue drink, which the children thought was delicious. Daniel was a little disappointed that Earth didn't provide this drink.

When they were finished, Cyrus packed the basket for the travelers to take with them.

"We thank you," said Pryn, bowing to Cyrus.

"It is my pleasure," said Cyrus. Turning now to Jennifer and Daniel, he added, "You are very special humans. I hope that this visit to my home has given you some ideas to work on when you return to your world. Do your part to make it a better world. If you do this, I will feel that my life's work is being accomplished."

Cyrus then shook hands with each of them, turned, and disappeared into his crystal home once more. Jennifer and Daniel were a bit sad when they realized that they would see no more of this special being.

Pryn could see this in their eyes. In his gentle

way, he reminded them of the purpose of their visit to Willowood. "We must continue our journey. There is still much to see and learn."

"We're really going to miss him," said Daniel.

Jennifer was very wistful. Taking Daniel's hand, she said, "Yes, we will miss Cyrus, but I feel that he has given us something. I don't know exactly how to describe it. It's like a gift somehow."

"A gift of the heart is what you mean," said Pryn with a small smile. He added, "You are indeed learning a great deal."

Nami led them down a set of crystal steps to their waiting boat. When they had boarded and arranged their knapsacks and basket of food, Pryn knocked three times on the bottom of the boat. Slowly they began to move. Nami jumped up and down on the bottom step. "Good-bye, I hope to see you again," Nami called to them in her reedy voice. They watched her tiny form disappear as she waved once more and dove into the water.

Perched high above them on top of his crystal home, Cyrus watched them as they continued their journey. "Good luck, my young friends. May all the Light that exists in the Universe shine on you forever. May it help you to win the battle that lies ahead."

His blue eyes were bright with tears as he uttered this prayer for them.

14.   LEELA'S PLACE

The crystals slowly disappeared from the banks of the stream. They stretched behind them like many scattered jewels and rainbows. The green foliage that took their place was different from the forest green of the Village. Large fernlike plants and strange trees could now be seen. There were dragonflies, brightly colored birds, and even some snakes. A delicate green mist was beginning to settle around them. It curled its way through the trees and plants, giving the scene a painted, watercolor look.

"Where are we now, Pryn?" asked Jennifer.

"It's sort of spooky around here," was Daniel's comment.

Pryn took a deep breath and looked around slowly. "This is Leela's Territory," he declared. Before the children could ask him, he explained, "Leela will help you to understand your thoughts and feelings about people and events in your life. She will teach you to see the good in everything and also to realize what is truly important and what is not."

Daniel had that puzzled look on his face again. He folded his arms and asked, "Am I going to understand any of this?"

Pryn smiled at the frowning little boy. "Have

you understood all that has happened so far?" he asked quietly.

"Well, yes, mostly everything." Daniel was surprised that this was indeed the case.

Then Jennifer took charge for the moment. "We're in this together. Whatever you don't understand, just ask me or Pryn."

Daniel gave his sister a hug. "I'm glad that you're my sister," he said, his small face beaming up at her.

Meanwhile, the atmosphere and surroundings were becoming more dense. Trees and plants were everywhere. There was a pleasant coolness in the air and a delightful fragrance also. Emerging from the heavy mist, a beautiful creature flew toward them. As it came closer, they could see that it was a butterfly. Its wings were pale green with a brilliant orange edging. There was one difference between this butterfly and any that Jennifer and Daniel had ever seen. This fantastic beauty was over two feet long.

The travelers were so amazed at the size of this butterfly that they never thought to ask Pryn about it. It landed gracefully on the front end of their boat, waving its wonderful wings.

"Should we give it something to eat?" asked Daniel. The children were delighted to be so close to this special creature.

"What does it want?" asked Jennifer.

"I think it will let us know," said Pryn in a soft, self-assured voice.

In a few moments, the butterfly flew on ahead of them. It flew high at times and circled above them. In a short while, it landed on the bank of the stream. The boat began to slow down and drift toward the bank. The butterfly had landed on white stone steps. A white stone path could be seen winding into the junglelike forest.

Pryn secured their boat, and they all stepped out onto the path. A few yards ahead and beside the path was a white pavilion with small wicker chairs and tables.

"Ah! I see a place where we can rest for a bit," said Pryn.

And so Jennifer, Daniel, and Pryn rested and ate a meal under this beautiful pavilion while the butterfly stayed on the steps watching and waving its wings. It was so dense in this part of Willowood that not much sun got through. The atmosphere of Leela's Territory was very mysterious.

15.   *LEELA*

When they had finished their meal and packed their belongings, Pryn, Jennifer, and Daniel stepped out of the pavilion and onto the white stone path. They felt refreshed, happy, and excited about their new adventure in Willowood.

"Where does Leela live?" asked Daniel.

Pryn answered in his soft voice, "At the end of the path." His golden eyes glowed with their special light.

Pryn took out his moonflute and started to hop and dance along the path. The butterfly circled above them, making swirls in the pale green mist. The forest was alive with sounds and scents that were strange and wonderful.

"Willowood certainly has a lot of different scenery," observed Jennifer as she looked around her.

Pryn glanced at her and replied, "Willowood can look any way that you can imagine." The sound of Pryn's moonflute blended perfectly with the forest sounds. The magic of Leela's territory was soothing to Jennifer and Daniel. They walked happily behind Pryn, feeling very much like they had always been here. Slowly, the path became wider. The children knew somehow that they were very close to Leela's place.

Pryn stopped and pointed ahead. The two young adventurers looked but could see only the green mist. Then, gradually, like a ghost that was beginning to materialize, they could see Leela's place.

"Look!" shouted Daniel.

"I see it too," said Jennifer very excitedly.

A large stone structure was becoming visible in front of them. It was made entirely of white stone, the same stone as the path they had walked along. It was a very different sort of house from anything that the children had ever seen. This house was two stories high. The first floor had a large doorway, which was rounded at the top. Many windows looked out on the forest. They too had rounded tops. The second level had a window on each side. Both the first and second levels of the house had six sides. The loveliest feature of this unusual home was the white stone of which it was made. Each stone was large and square with a surface so smooth that it looked like glass. This is what Jennifer and Daniel saw standing before them.

"What a beautiful house!" exclaimed Jennifer, walking closer to it. Daniel was right behind her.

"Where is Leela?" he asked Pryn.

Pryn was watching his two companions with a small smile on his face. "I'm sure that we will see her soon."

It was as if Leela had heard Pryn because she appeared in the doorway at that moment. The children were startled at the appearance of this new friend in their adventure. Leela was very beautiful. She was a little taller than Jennifer with long black hair and large dark eyes. When she smiled at them, they could see beautiful white teeth. Leela's skin was a lovely bronze color. She wore a long white tunic and white sandals. Around her throat was a necklace made of tiny stones of every color.

The mist seemed to clear around Leela's house, and a pale sunlight glittered on the polished stone. She walked toward them with her arms outstretched and spoke to them.

"Hello, my precious ones. I am Leela."

16.   *LEELA'S STORY*

It seemed to Jennifer and Daniel that they had known Leela for a long time. Something about her voice was so familiar. They each took one of her hands as she walked them into her home. Pryn followed behind them.

The inside of Leela's home was just as unusual as the outside. All of her furniture was made of the same white polished stone. The floors were like mirrors. Here and there were large stone containers with beautiful green plants in them. The white walls, however, were inlaid with brilliant mosaics. These mosaics depicted unusual scenes. The visitors were quite puzzled by these pictures.

Daniel stepped in front of one mosaic. "I can't figure out this picture," he said to Leela. "Is it a car, a plane, or a bus? Everything looks different." He turned to Leela for an answer.

She was sitting at a low bench, smiling at the little boy. "I don't think that you will recognize very much in these scenes." As she spoke, her sweeping gesture indicated all of the pictures adorning her walls.

Jennifer sat on the bench beside Leela. "Pryn told us that we are here to learn and that he would help us to understand things."

"That's right," agreed Daniel, looking at Pryn for a sign of approval. Pryn was perched on a small bench nearby. He smiled at Daniel and nodded slowly.

Leela stood up. She looked intently at the picture that puzzled Daniel. "Pryn is right, of course," she said to them. "I was waiting to see if you would ask me. You have not disappointed me." She began to explain in her firm, musical voice. "These pictures tell the story of a land that no longer exists. They show how the people lived and what happened to them. Perhaps you can learn a lesson from their story."

"Did their sun die out?" asked Daniel, thinking he would be treated to another outer space story.

"No," said Leela, "but for these people, the result was the same. They were a very advanced race of people who had great power. But they misused this power and destroyed themselves."

"How did they do that?" Daniel wanted to know.

Leela took his hand and walked to another scene. This picture was a sad one. It showed one man forcing another to carry a heavy load. Leela's voice became very serious. "Some of the people mistreated others who were not as fortunate. They kept them as slaves. However, many good people did not like this practice. They could not settle their disagreement peaceably, and a great war followed. Because they were very smart, their weapons were very powerful. This war destroyed their land, causing it to sink into the ocean."

The children now stood in front of a very large

picture. In this picture, enormous waves covered the land. It was a chilling sight. "Did all the people sink with the land?" asked Jennifer with tears in her eyes.

"Not all of them," answered Leela with a sigh. "Some of them could tell that trouble was on the way. They escaped in large ships to different parts of the Earth."

The children's eyes grew large. "Did you say the Earth?" they asked in unison.

Leela was silent for a moment. Her head was bowed, and her face was hidden by her beautiful hair. "Yes," she answered them in a whisper, "our own Earth." She looked at them and smiled sadly.

Holding out her hands to them, she said, "Come with me." Leela led them to a mosaic that they hadn't seen yet. In this picture, they could see three people seated on a bench much like the ones in Leela's home. They all had black hair and eyes and wore tunics.

It was Daniel who noticed that the middle person was Leela. He turned slowly and said in a small voice. "This is you, Leela, isn't it?"

Leela smiled at his serious face and nodded. "Yes, Daniel, that is a picture of me with my mother and father. They were very good people who tried to help the unfortunate ones. They put me on a ship to safety, but they stayed behind to help as many people as possible. When Atlantis sank they were still there."

Leela gazed at the picture for a while. "It has been a long, long time since that day, but I still miss them very much," she said softly.

Daniel took her hand, and looking up at her,

said, "I'm sorry you're still sad." Leela smiled at him and guided him to a small group of benches. Jennifer and Pryn sat on a bench facing them.

Leela began to speak. "You are both quite young, but as you grow older, you will notice how many kinds of people are in your world. Many people are very poor. They are so poor that they have nothing to eat, no clothes to wear, and nowhere to live. These people rely on others to help them out."

"How can we help them?" asked Jennifer. "I don't think we have very much money." It was at this moment in her life that Jennifer first realized her family's situation.

"Are we poor, Jenny?" asked Daniel, his eyes growing large in his small, bewildered face.

"I'm not sure," said Jennifer. She was a little puzzled.

It was Pryn who answered their question. "Your family possesses a large fortune when it comes to love and happiness," he said softly, "but money is very scarce."

"How do you know that?" asked a curious Daniel.

Pryn drew his knees to his chin and lowered his lids over his golden eyes. "I know all about you," he said with a smile.

Leela rose from the bench and walked slowly around the room. She continued, "There are many kinds of poverty," she said. "You are special children because you will be in a unique position to help others."

"Why?" they both asked her.

"Because of your own poverty, you will become aware of those even less fortunate. You will both always want to help them. Your opportunity will come as you become adults and your childhood dreams become realities. Many people dream, but very few have come here to Willowood. Only those who believe in their dreams and whose dreams are filled with love come here."

The children sat silently, trying to understand Leela's words. They were overwhelmed and a little afraid of what seemed a very big responsibility to the future.

Suddenly, Jennifer remembered what Pryn told them about changing their dream. She stood up and said in a firm voice, "I am not afraid, and I do understand."

Daniel stood up beside her. "Me too!" he said. With those words came a warm glow of joy and love and strength that they had never felt before.

"Please tell us more about Atlantis," said Daniel. Pryn and Leela smiled at each other and then at Jennifer and Daniel.

"Of course, I'll tell you more," she said. "I have many murals and many stories to go with them."

Night was coming to Leela's territory. As it became darker, the walls of Leela's home started to glow with a soft white light. The murals seemed to take on a life of their own in this light. Leela spent many hours with the children. She told them the story of Atlantis from beginning to end. She was proud of her people's achievements and sorry for their downfall. But in her stories there were many lessons for the visitors. They asked many questions and acquired a deep understanding of human dignity. They became aware of the uniqueness and preciousness of each human being.

Daniel was especially impressed with the story of Atlantis. He felt that his favorite outer space stories had come to Earth after all. "Did they really have spaceships and cars that floated on air?" he asked in a voice filled with awe.

"Yes, they did have them and much more," answered Leela. It gave her great pleasure to tell about her lost home.

"How did you come to live in Willowood?" asked Jennifer.

"Ah!" said Pryn, "a very good question."

Leela smiled at Pryn. Her answer was not an easy one to understand, but somewhere in their hearts, the children knew it was true.

"My journeys on the Earth are now finished," Leela said, fixing her eyes on Jennifer and Daniel. "The part of me that is forever has chosen to reside in Willowood and help those who will benefit from my experiences on Earth."

An idea began to form in Jennifer's mind. "Where do you go when you need help?" she asked. "Is there a Willowood for you and Pryn and the others who live here?"

Leela was surprised at this question, but not Pryn.

"I told you that these are very special children,"

he said to Leela in his soft voice. His eyes were shining in the pale light. He was very pleased with Jennifer's question.

Once again Leela took Jennifer and Daniel by the hand. "Yes, there is a place for us," she said very seriously. "It is a place within each of us where there is only light and joy and perfect peace. Much of our time is spent there. When we sense that a soul may need us, we return here to Willowood to help. We are the protectors of those who dream and seek the knowledge to make those dreams a reality."

"Can we ever go to the perfect place?" asked Daniel as he tightened his grip on Leela's hand.

"Yes, you can," she answered, smiling into his intent little face. "You are already on your way to finding it."

In the moment of silence that followed, Jennifer and Daniel realized just how much they had come to love Leela. They both hugged her now and as the first light of morning began to filter through the mist. "My precious ones," she whispered. Pryn gathered their things together as Leela walked the children to the door of her home. "It is time for you to begin the final trip of your journey in Willowood," she said. "You must remember everything that you have learned here to pass the test of the Great Castle. Go with love and courage in your hearts. If you pass the final test, you will always remember the dream that is Willowood."

Jennifer and Daniel wished that they could stay with Leela a little longer, but in their hearts they knew she was right. The beautiful butterfly was circling overhead. When it started to fly toward the river, the trio began their trek back to the waiting boat. The children turned to wave good-bye, but all that was there was the dense, swirling mist.

Leela had gone back to her place of perfect peace.

17.   *THE GREAT CASTLE*

Very gradually the stream began to widen. The air turned colder and heavier. The tropical atmosphere of Leela's territory was giving way to a much different climate. A pale orange sun was streaked with wispy purple clouds. It cast a golden orange glow on the huge oak trees that were beginning to line the banks of the stream. A smoky, autumnlike scent was in the air.

The small craft was nearing another bend in its journey downstream. Two of its passengers were not aware that this was the final turn they would make.

Jennifer and Daniel talked with Pryn for many hours about the friends they had made in Willowood and what they had learned from them. A growing sense of anticipation was now stirring in the children.

"What did Leela mean about passing a test?" Jennifer asked Pryn. Daniel moved closer to his big sister, letting Pryn know that he had the same question.

Pryn smiled at his two young companions. In a quiet, serious voice he said, "I think it is time to prepare you both for your visit to the Great Castle." Two pairs of intense eyes were upon him.

"The Queen of Willowood is called Mariel. She has reigned for many ages. But another force dwells within the Great Castle. He is called the Nameless One."

"Why doesn't he have a name?" asked Daniel.

"Because he can be many things," answered Pryn, with a smile and a wink at the little boy. "He can look like a man or a woman. He can be be a thought or a feeling—but always a negative one."

"What is negative?" asked Jennifer.

"Ah! A good question," Pryn answered softly. "Negative feelings are anger and hate, sadness, unhappiness, also sickness and death. The Nameless One is the absence of all light. Light is positive and happy. Life in all its forms." Jennifer and Daniel were silent for a moment.

Then Jennifer asked, "Will we meet the Nameless One?"

"Oh, yes," said Pryn. "You will meet both Mariel and the Nameless One. Are you afraid?" he asked them.

Little Daniel thought again about his journey through Willowood. He folded his arms, and in his bravest voice, he said, "I'm not afraid of anything!"

Jennifer laughed at Daniel's stern little face, then put her arm around him and turned to Pryn. "If Daniel's not afraid, then neither am I."

Pryn's eyes sparkled in the orange sunlight. He smiled at them and said, "I am very proud of you both."

The stream began to turn just as the sun began

to set on Willowood. The navigator fish were sparkling under their little boat. Pryn was playing his moonflute, and the children were admiring the beautiful scene. Without any warning, the stream led into an enormous waterway—The River. Jennifer and Daniel sat up straight in amazement. Their small boat came to a slow stop. They watched as the navigator fish swam away.

"What's happening?" asked Jennifer.

Pryn gently laid down his moonflute and said softly, "We have come to The River. From now on your desires will lead the way, so we no longer need our little navigators. Where do you want to go?"

They replied in unison, "To the Great Castle." They began to move again. For the first time on their journey, they could see other boats. Some were large with many lights. Others were small like their own. In the fading glow of the sun, they could also see strange planes and ships in the sky. Pryn answered their unspoken question. "Willowood exists for everyone in the Universe."

The excitement and anticipation of the children carried the small craft at a steady pace. And their excitement grew as the purple and orange glow of sunset became dotted with crystal stars. Jennifer and Daniel wished for eyes that could see even more. Immediately their surroundings became sharper and clearer, as if a film were cleared from their eyes. With this newfound clarity, objects that were quite far away became visible.

"Pryn," said Jennifer in a low voice, "look at

that purple star up ahead. It's so big and it looks like it's sitting right on the water."

"I see it too," said Daniel, drawing closer to his sister.

Pryn sighed a sigh of awe and said, "What you see is the very top of the Great Castle. It is a purple crystal, which glows continuously. Queen Mariel lives within this glow."

"Where does the Nameless One live?" asked Daniel.

"Ah!" Pryn murmured in a quiet and serious tone. "He dwells in the deepest pit of the Great Castle below the water itself."

"Can he ever get out?" asked Jennifer in a worried voice.

"Yes—if we let him," was Pryn's answer.

"We won't ever let him out," said Daniel.

Pryn smiled at Daniel, and his golden eyes sparkled. "The word 'we' does not only mean us or even all the human race, but every living creature in the Universe." Daniel's eyes were wide with wonder. "Queen Mariel will explain more when you arrive," Pryn added.

The night was clear and crisp. The stars sparkled with crystalline brilliance. The children were filled with many emotions. Excitement, anticipation, curiosity, and a little bit of apprehension combined in their minds and bodies, making them even more attentive. The purple crystal glowed brighter and grew larger as they drew nearer to it. Pryn was no longer playing his moonflute. A different kind of music was filling their minds and hearts.

The travelers continued to watch the strange ships in the sky as they took on more definition in the first light of dawn. They noticed that part of the sky remained black. In a few moments, they realized that they were looking at the Great Castle.

There are no words that could truly describe the majestic and incredible Great Castle. Only the eyes of a dream can really see such beauty. The River became so wide that it could no longer be described as a river, but as an ocean. No longer could they see trees or land of any kind. Directly in front of them, but still some distance away, a gigantic mountain of rock jutted from the ocean floor to the sky itself. Huge waves lapped against its solid sides. It was a dark rock—almost black—with many angles and outcroppings shining in the sun. About one hundred feet from the top of the Castle, the dark rock seemed to melt into the purple-violet crystal.

Many entryways dotted the Castle where it was level with the water. Some very large entryways were higher up, and spaceships could be seen coming and going from them.

"This is great!" said Daniel, his voice filled with wonder and excitement. "It's even better than any outer space book I've read." Pryn smiled at the little boy. He had never seen anyone so young who did not fear the ancient Castle.

Jennifer was also smiling at Daniel, but her face was more serious and thoughtful. "I wonder what Queen Mariel is like," she mused.

"You will soon find out," said Pryn softly.

Their desire to get inside the Great Castle was propelling the little boat at a great speed. Soon they came to a halt in front of a large opening in the rock. To their astonishment, a bird as large as a man stepped out to greet them. The bird was black with red, piercing eyes. Around his neck was a medallion very much like Jennifer and Daniel's except that it was purple in color.

The bird bowed to them and said, "You must give me your medallions as a pass." The children quickly took off their medallions and handed them to the bird. The large creature then stood back, and they began to move inside the Great Castle.

"I've never seen a talking bird," said Jennifer.

"Me either," echoed Daniel, looking over his shoulder at the tall guard. But they had come to accept the many strange happenings in Willowood as normal.

They found themselves inside a large cavern. It was lit by a bright torch set into the wall. Other than this light, there was nothing at all in the room. They got out of their boat, stepped onto the rock floor of the cavern, and looked around them.

Finally, Jennifer asked Pryn, "How do we get to see Queen Mariel from here?"

Pryn laughed softly, his eyes flickering with the light. "Each of you take my hand," he said. The three of them were now standing in a small circle. "Remember what I have told you. Your thoughts and desires will take you to your destination. Where do you wish to go?"

Jennifer and Daniel looked at each other. They closed their eyes and said together, "We wish to see Queen Mariel." A strong wind seemed to rush by them. For a moment they felt as if they were suspended in mid-air. When they felt something solid under their feet again, they opened their eyes.

18. QUEEN MARIEL

Deep purple-violet crystal surrounded them. It sparkled above them and under their feet. It filled their minds and hearts with a glowing strength and a sense of peace and joy. They were in the chamber of Mariel—Queen of Willowood.

She was seated on a beautiful purple crystal throne in the center of the chamber. "Come to me, my little seekers." Mariel's voice was like a delicate wind chime—light and clear. What a dazzling sight she was. Mariel's eyes were light blue. Her hair was a pale gold light glowing around her face. She appeared to have a white robe draped around her. The robe glittered with every color imaginable. When she stood to greet them, the colors changed and rippled. Mariel was composed of light patterns that took on a human form.

They stood before her now, and her beauty surrounded them. Pryn bowed his deepest bow and said, "I have brought two souls who wish to know you."

To which Mariel replied, "And they shall know me, for I am their highest potential. If they choose me to fill their hearts with my light, they will help their world to attain its rightful place in the Universe."

Jennifer took Daniel's hand and spoke to the Queen. "We do want to help, but we're not sure what to do. Pryn said that you can help us."

Mariel sat down again and pulled the children close to her. Her touch was like a warm tingling on their skin. Her brilliant eyes melted their fears and absorbed their attention. The words she spoke would remain in their hearts forever.

"You must make a choice," she began, "I am the light that fills your world and all the Universe with goodness, peace, harmony, and joy. I am the true wealth of life. My light brings the only real happiness. But there are times when this light is hard to see. The Nameless One can show you a false light, an easy way. Those who choose this way fall into a pit of darkness from which it may take countless ages to return. You must keep my image in your hearts always. If you do this, then the temptations of the Nameless One will never sway you. But if you cannot resist him, you will forget your dream of Willowood and struggle on with the rest of your life. He will become stronger in the Universe if the light in your hearts cannot subdue him."

"Are we strong enough to fight the Nameless One?" whispered Daniel. "Is this the test we have to pass?"

Mariel replied, "Your souls would never have sought this dream if you were not strong enough. Your own strength added to what you have learned on this journey will be more than enough to win the battle. You must face him now or forever lose the dream." Mariel leaned forward and kissed each of them. The purple chamber began to fade away, and the light that was Mariel grew to a dazzling brilliance before it was gone.

They were in the cavern again, the little boat still bobbing in the water.

Pryn said in a sad and quiet voice, "I must leave you now. My purpose has been fulfilled." The little elf bowed to them.

"We love you, Pryn," said Daniel sadly.

"I hope we see you again someday," said Jennifer. She gave Pryn a big hug.

Pryn smiled and blushed. "I will always be here for you."

Jennifer and Daniel watched as their beloved Pryn climbed into the boat that had carried them so far. Tears filled their eyes as he disappeared from view.

19. *THE NAMELESS ONE*

Two small figures stood in the torchlit cave. They looked small and fragile. No casual observer would guess the strength that their hearts and souls possessed.

"Are you ready, Daniel?" asked Jennifer in a clear and steady voice.

"I'm ready," he replied.

Hand in hand, and with eyes tightly shut, they said together, "We wish to meet the Nameless One!"

The floor of the cavern melted away, and again they felt a floating sensation. When they stood on solid ground again, they opened their eyes. Their new surroundings leapt at them from all directions. The children found themselves in a gigantic cavern of red stone. It felt warm to them, and had a very sour smell.

"I don't like this place," whispered Daniel.

"Me either," echoed Jennifer. "I wonder what that is."

She pointed to a circle of white light that illuminated the cavern. The children walked toward this strange light very slowly. It was eerily quiet in this place. As they drew nearer to the circle, the light began to brighten until they stood at the very edge.

"Who seeks to enter my home?" a deep and silky

voice asked them. Jennifer and Daniel were so startled that they ran back several steps and clung to each other. "Ha, ha, ha," the voice chuckled quietly. "Come closer, little ones. Are you afraid?"

"No! We're not," answered Jennifer in a small, shaky voice. From the center of the circle, a large shadow rose. It had the shape of a man, but it had no substance. It was the blackest shadow imaginable. When the children looked at him, they were seeing absolute nothingness—the absence of the light. They were confronted by the Nameless One.

Jennifer and Daniel crept a little closer to the circle. Again the light became brighter. They realized that the Nameless One could not cross the circle of light.

"As you can see, I am a prisoner of Mariel's light."

The shadowy voice was very easy to listen to. It was a soothing voice, and it calmed the children's fear.

"He doesn't seem so scary to me," Daniel whispered to his sister.

"I know," she replied, "but let's be careful anyway."

The Nameless One seated himself cross-legged in the center of the circle. The smooth voice spoke to them again. "The good Queen could never understand how I feel about things. Instead of letting me try my ideas, she keeps me in this dungeon. Do you think this is fair?"

Jennifer asked him, "What are you ideas?"

The Nameless One reached toward them slightly and said, "I'm so glad you asked me that question.

Maybe you can help me. I want only to make things easier for the human race."

"How can you do that?" Daniel wanted to know.

"Ah ha!" The Nameless One stood up again. "I can help by helping everyone to help themselves. Is that so hard to understand?"

But Jennifer saw a trap, and she questioned the Nameless One. "What about helping other people?"

The deep voice became louder and said, "Why should you help anyone else? If everyone helped themselves, there would be no need to help another."

"But there are people so poor and hungry that they can't do anything about it," Daniel said,, remembering what Leela told them.

"Ahhhhhh!" screamed the huge shadow, "If they are that poor, then the world would be better off without them, and there would be more for you." The children considered this for a moment, and during that time the circle of light grew dim. The Nameless One crept closer to the edge of the circle, and his voice grew soft again.

"Don't you see that my idea make sense?"

"No!" cried Daniel, thinking of how it would feel to be very hungry all of the time or to be cold and have nothing to wear. "I'm always going to help other people."

Immediately the circle of light became brighter, and the Nameless One had to move back into the center again. "Oh well," he mused softly, "not everyone sees eye to eye on everything. But I have many good ideas."

The Nameless One was quiet for a moment. Then he spoke again in a voice full of promise. "Your family is very poor, isn't it? Wouldn't you like to help your parents?"

Jennifer and Daniel looked at each other. They loved their parents very much. It wouldn't hurt to listen to what this being had to say. The circle dimmed ever so slightly.

"What can we do?" asked Jennifer cautiously.

"Oh, you are a smart little girl," the silky voice replied. "It is possible that your father could work somewhere else where his salary would be much higher."

"Where is that?" asked Daniel.

The Nameless One's voice became jubilant. "There is a place that makes something very important. Your father's help would be welcome there. I can arrange that, but you must agree to my plan. That's simple enough, isn't it?"

Daniel whispered to his sister. "Daddy works so hard. Maybe we should agree." The circle of light was becoming even more dim.

Jennifer noticed this and said to Daniel, "Something is wrong. We have to think about it." She explained to Daniel, "It's the light of Queen Mariel that keeps him in here, but look how dark it's getting. This must be part of the test." All at once her face brightened. "I have an idea." She took Daniel's hand and whispered again, "Just keep holding on to me." Daniel looked up at her and smiled a very little smile.

While they spoke, the creature of shadows was

humming to himself. When he saw that they were watching him again, he said, "Well? Won't it be nice to have lots of toys?"

"Wait," said Jennifer firmly, "we haven't agreed to anything yet. My brother and I would like to know what our Dad would be helping to make."

The shadowy voice grew loud and angry. "Who cares? You would have a nice house and anything you could wish for. Why ask questions?"

"We have to know," said Daniel.

"As you wish. Your father would be helping to make weapons for soldiers. These are much needed in times like these."

Daniel remembered what Leela had said about the powerful weapons of her people. "Weapons and war can hurt people," he cried.

"And destroy whole countries," added Jennifer. "No! We won't agree to your plan."

The circle of light glowed intensely. The Nameless One screamed and waved his fists in the air. "Ahhhhh! I don't need you to agree. I'll do it without your help. There are millions in the universe who see the wisdom of my ideas."

In the emptiness of his being, the children could see the dark images of wartorn cities and homeless people. Hunger and suffering were everywhere. They saw how their environment would change. Plants and animals would die, and, finally, all the Earth would become a wasteland.

Jennifer and Daniel watched these images with horror. But with this feeling came an understanding

of all that they had learned in Willowood. The words of Pryn, Cyrus, Leela, and Mariel combined in their minds and hearts to give them power and strength. They knew what must be done.

"This is only a dream!" Jennifer shouted. "And we can change it."

"How will you do that?" the Nameless One screamed the question and laughed wildly. "How can you fight me?"

"By helping others all of our lives," said Daniel.

"And by helping the whole world become a good place to live now and as we grow up," said Jennifer.

Finally, in one voice, they said, "We are changing this dream."

Slowly the Nameless One began to fade. The noise created by his images faded with him. They were surrounded by a dazzling light. Mariel appeared before them. "You have passed the test. The dream is yours forever." The crystal voice faded away. Her eyes became two of the millions of crystal stars that surrounded them.

Jennifer opened her eyes. She saw their small bedroom with its cracked ceiling and faded peeling wallpaper. Daniel ran to her bed.

"We're home, we're home!" he was shouting with happiness and excitement.

"Yes, Daniel"—she was hugging him tightly— we're home.

20.   *AFTERWORD*

It was autumn again. The trees were many brilliant and splendid colors against a sky that promised an early winter. The wind gave the fallen leaves a life of their own as they skipped and danced across the large field. Autumn. Mysterious, smoky fragrances lingered in the breezes triggering a profusion of thoughts and feelings in most human beings.

Two children ran and shouted and played wildly in a field bordering a small forest. Worn-out jackets flapped about their slim figures. The lights of surrounding farmhouses began to twinkle through the trees.

A woman watched them play through a small kitchen window. The children called her Mommy. She loved them so very much. It was almost dinnertime in the old farmhouse. Mommy was waiting for their father to return before calling them in for wash-up and dinner. She stood at the window, watching and thinking of all that had happened in the past year. A job for her husband that enabled them to move to the country. They were still quite poor, but never were they so happy. The biggest change, she thought, was in her children. They had grown in mind, body, and spirit in a sudden burst that seemed to take place overnight. Their eagerness to learn and

willingness to help became an amazing joy to her and to their father.

Her children! They were special. She always knew they would be. And now, as she gazed at the deepening sky, she saw a large star glittering like a perfect crystal. A knowing smile stole across her face. She winked at the star, causing a tear to trickle down her cheek. No one could hear the simple prayer that she uttered to the sky. "Thank you . . . thank you!"